THE CRABS ON CALHOUN

Enjoy the adventure!
Katherine

Bardolf & Company
Sarasota, Florida

The CRABS on CALHOUN

ISBN# 978-1-938842-58-0
Copyright © 2022
by Katherine Robinson

Cover and interior layout by Bardolf & Company

Dedicated to the charming, quirky,
wonderful and beautiful people,
past, present and future,
who call Bluffton home.
Their history, stories, and "state of mind"
have kept me in this delightful, eclectic, and
quintessential southern town
which all helped create
The Crabs on Calhoun!

Blessings, laughter, and joy
to all who read this book.

bluffton
HEART OF THE LOWCOUNTRY

Situated on a natural bluff overlooking the May River, Old Town Bluffton is filled with wonderful boutiques, antebellum homes, historic churches, treasure-filled antique shops, beautiful parks, caffeine rich cafés, great restaurants, art galleries and so much more. Southern hospitality is always in style here.

The Town of Bluffton was settled in 1825 and officially incorporated in 1852. More than a century later during the Civil War in the summer of 1863, it was almost completely destroyed when Federal troops arrived from Savannah and burned the Town down. Only eight antebellum houses and two churches survived.

For many years the one-square-mile area that includes Calhoun Street, known as Old Town Bluffton, comprised the entire town. In the last 25 years, a number of annexations of surrounding residential areas have occurred, which has increased the size of the town to more than 54 square miles. The Town has done a great job of blending the old with new construction to create a pleasant, unified atmosphere.

The Crabs on Calhoun

By Katherine Robinson

Illustrated by Jacob Eaton

Bluffton, South Carolina, known as "the Heart of the Lowcountry," is uniquely positioned between Savannah, Georgia, Hilton Head Island and Charleston, South Carolina. Lying on the May River, it is a beautiful place with historic buildings, funky galleries, tree-lined streets and docks on the river. There is lots of marine life, too.

Among them are 10 Fiddler Crabs. You can see them on the cover. From left to right, their names are FULTON, FELIX, FALALA, FREDDY, FLETCHER, FRANNY, FERGUSON, FELICIA, and FRANKLIN, with their teacher, MR. FINNEGAN behind them. They all love to play and go on adventures. Sometimes, when they've done really well with their homework or finish their schoolwork early, their teacher, Mr. Finnegan, lets them go into the Old Town Bluffton Historic District to play their favorite game: Hide and Go Seek!

One day in Art Class, FaLaLa decided to make bronze Fiddler Crab sculptures of herself and her classmates, and their teacher. The next time they all went into Bluffton, they put them near their favorite hiding places along Calhoun Street and in Dubois Park. Even Mr. Finnegan picked out a place for himself. Some of them are easy to spot, others require some searching.

They hope that you will try to find them. In the following pages, you will find some clues about each one, along with some interesting information about the location where each Fiddler Crab is hidden. Plus, there are some nifty tidbits about Fiddler Crabs for you to learn too!

There is also additional information for your parents, teachers, and others who would like to take a walking tour of the Old Town Bluffton area and surrounding attractions. In fact, if you contact the author, she might just lead your tour!

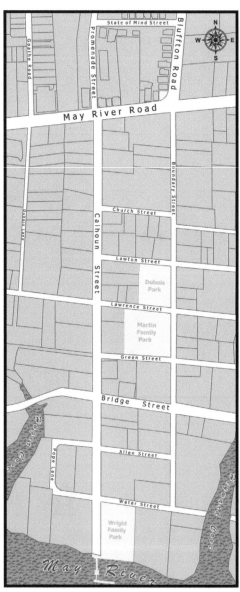

Downtown Bluffton

There is another map on a separate card for you to use. Write your name beside each Fiddler Crab as you find it and, when complete, bring your card to the Heyward House Museum and Welcome Center in Bluffton or the Town Hall for a special surprise! The Heyward House is located at 70 Boundary Street and Town Hall is located at 20 Bridge Street.

You can start anywhere along Calhoun Street, but the book follows the path which begins at the dock by the river and the large sign nearby telling more about the Fiddlers on Calhoun.

Calhoun Street Dock

If you get stuck trying to find one of the Fiddlers, just ask your parent or teacher—they can help you!

Are you ready to join in the search for the Fiddler Crabs in the pages ahead? If so, call out "Come out, come out, wherever you are," and begin!

Ready? Set? Go!

FRANKLIN is the first Fiddler Crab you can try to find.

Franklin loves the water, and his favorite subject in school is Marine Biology. He really likes finding shells, watching dolphins swim in the May River, and seeing all the birds flying around, like great blue herons, egrets, and kingfishers.

Here are some clues for you to find Franklin:

 Franklin can see the May River from where he's hiding.

 Franklin enjoys a view of the Calhoun Street Dock and The Church of the Cross.

 Franklin is next to the beautiful Wright Family Park.

FUN FACT

Did you know that only boy Fiddler Crabs have the big claw?
This is what they use to wave at the girl Fiddler Crabs they want to meet.

The sculpture of Franklin sits on a pole next to the Wright Family Park and the Calhoun Street Dock, which provides great, panoramic views of Bluffton's marine treasure: the May River. Many boaters love to spend time on the water. Often you can see Captain Amber, owner of Spartina Marine Education Charters, giving tours that are like scientific expeditions of the area.

Take a walk around the park and you'll see a few spots where you can read signboards about the Wright Family and their history. The Town of Bluffton placed a swing on one of the large trees on the property. Take a moment to sit and swing and enjoy the view. You are steps away from the May River where you might pick up an oyster shell and likely spot some fiddler crabs scurrying around. The Squire Pope Cottage, which is located on the Wright Family Park property, was built in 1850 and is currently being restored.

While you are there, be sure to walk around the Church of the Cross and look up high. You will probably spot some bees buzzing around near the church bell. The Church of the Cross gives them a home and sells "Holy Honey!"

Construction started in 1855 and the first service was held on July 17, 1857. The church was made entirely of long leaf pine on brick piers. Inside, some windows still have the original pink glass panes from England. The English pipe organ in the loft was installed in 1999. According to a postcard dated March 1907, during the Civil War when Union soldiers burned Bluffton, they were ordered not to destroy this old church. Some days, a docent offers guided tours of the church's interior. The Church of the Cross was listed on the National Register of Historic places on May 29, 1975.

Views of the May River from the bluff near the church are always pictures that become postcard worthy. Sunset views are stunning and weddings, proms and other special occasions are often posed here. The May River is an integral part of Bluffton and has helped define the Town's history. Views of the lovely May River add to the quality of life for the citizens and visitors of Bluffton.

FELICIA is the next Fiddler Crab for you to find.

Felicia is a Girl Scout who loves to help people. She already has earned her "Celebrating Community" badge and is working on her "Inside Government" badge. Felicia would love to work for the Town of Bluffton when she grows up and maybe even become Mayor some day! Her favorite time of year is when she gets to sell Girl Scout Cookies, especially Do-Si-Dos and Thin Mints.

Here are some clues to help you find Felicia:

 You have to look up high to see Felicia.

 Felicia can see the Bluffton United Methodist Church from her favorite hiding place.

 You can park your car or bike near where she helps point the way to the Public Dock, Historic Register Site, Town Hall and the Visitors Center.

FUN FACT

Did you know that Fiddler Crabs can change colors,
from coral red, bright green, yellow, or blue?
In the daytime they take on dark colors, and in the night they are more pale.

As you walk north on Calhoun Street and just past Water Street, you'll find Fiddler Crab Felicia's sculpture on a tall, yellow sign post.

So much to see from Felicia's post!

Across the street from her post is the Bluffton United Methodist Church. It was built on its current location around 1890.

In 1940, a category 2 hurricane came ashore in Beaufort and the people of Bluffton experienced the wrath of this storm, too. In his article "Almost Forgotten History of Bluffton's United Methodist Church" John Samuel Graves, III wrote, "The Methodist Church was completely demolished by one of these [oak trees], the whole center crushed leaving the altar exposed at one end and the steeple slanting at the other with the faithful old bell poised visibly as though to ring prophetically the last call to prayer."

This part of Calhoun Street is also home to "Seven Oaks," which was built around 1860. For some time in the 1920s, it was a popular boarding house.

Located just north of Seven Oaks is the Fripp-Lowden Lowcountry cottage, built in 1909 (*below left*).

And, across the street are two places for you to check out for shopping and other activities. The Moonlit Lullaby, with the crab above the second-floor porch, has wonderful presents for small children. May River Excursions has a great gift shop and offers all kinds of local tours and fishing expeditions.

The next Fiddler Crab to find is FELIX.

Felix loves gardening and is always digging in the pluff mud after tending to the spartina grass that grows in the marsh. He almost always has a shovel or watering can in his claw to help Farmer B take care of the gardens at the May River Montessori.

Here are some clues to help you find Fiddler Crab Felix:

 Felix is hanging around a busy place. When you find him, he can help direct you to places like The Sippin Cow, Oyster Factory Park, The Heyward House, Town Hall, St John Church, Pritchard Street Park, and Campbell AME Church"

 Felix can see Calhoun Street and the May River Montessori front yard garden from his hiding place. During springtime, you'll notice kale, broccoli, spinach and strawberries growing in the school's garden for the children to pick and taste.

 Felix is located next to three buildings called The Bridge at Calhoun.

FUN 🦀 FACT

Fiddler Crabs like to dig holes or burrows to sleep in
and give them a place to hide if someone is coming around.

Keep walking north on Calhoun for Fiddler Crab Felix's sculpture on a signpost pointing the way to a lot of places where he can hide. They include Bluffton Town Hall, the Heyward House Museum and Welcome Center, St John's Church, Pritchard Street's Pocket Park, Sippin' Cow Café, Oyster Factory Park, and Campbell AME Church.

The Bridge at Calhoun is a new vibrant mixed-use hub of three buildings on the corner of the Bridge and Calhoun intersection—with retail shops and a restaurant to come in 2022.

If you happen to be visiting on a Thursday afternoon, check out the award winning Farmer's Market down the street at the Martin Family Park. It features seasonal fresh, local produce, plants, honey, eggs, beef and seafood, along with specialty items and prepared foods. On Thursday's the Farmer's Market is a must!

The author and her sister, Charlene, at the Farmer's Market.

Across Calhoun Street from Felix's signpost is May River Montessori— "Entrusted with Bluffton's children since 1987." The school has one of the most beautiful flower and vegetable gardens in the area just past the sidewalk and fence.

Fiddler Crab FULTON has so much fun in his hiding spot! Fulton loves photography and takes his best pictures with his "shell" phone. Fulton's Mom taught him how to take "shellfies" and he is often seen smiling and hoping someone will come by and join him for a picture.

Here are some clues to help you find Fulton:

 From his favorite spot, Fulton can see The Store, La Petite Gallerie, High Tide Beads, and the Calhoun Street Gallery.

 Fulton can also see The Pearl Restaurant across the street.

 Fulton's sculpture is on a short post ready to pose with you. You can sit down next to Fulton and have a "shellfie" taken with him!

FUN 🦀 FACT

Fiddler Crabs are busy creatures—always eating, digging, scurrying around.
Never a still moment for them!

As you continue to stroll north on Calhoun, look to the left at the corner of Lawrence Street. This is where you will find Fiddler Crab Fulton's sculpture occupying a special spot atop a metal column just behind a park bench. If you feel like it, you can have a seat, take a break, and look around.

There are interesting shops and restaurants nearby on Calhoun Street. Just to the north is the Camellia Art and Framing Shop (*pictured below*). The historic single-family home was built around 1947 and was remodeled to operate a a retail store and art gallery. Across the Street is The Pearl Restaurant with inspired coastal cuisine utilizing some of the best fresh-catch seafood and local produce available.

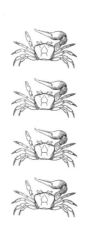

Make sure you visit GiGi's and the Red Piano Art Gallery nearby.

In Babbie Guscio's shop, called The Store, you can always find a special treasure. Built in 1904, this one-and-a-half story frame building has a weatherboard exterior giving it a unique look that just begs you to walk in a see what's inside. Behind the fiddler crab is the Calhoun Street Gallery with things that are unique, beautiful and unexpected.

Nearby is the Old Town Dispensary Restaurant (*pictured left*), where good friends, cold drinks and delicious food come together. You can dine outside, a perfect spot for people watching on Calhoun Street.

Fiddler Crabs FRANNY and FREDDY are twins and decided to find hiding places close to each other just off Calhoun Street in Dubois Park on their favorite playground in Bluffton. They both love sports. Franny plays softball with a group of other fiddler crabs. She is the pitcher on her team. Freddy is crazy about soccer and plays the goalkeeper, stopping balls with his large claw.

Here are some clues to help you find Franny and Freddy:

 You have to look up high to see them, but they are not together.

 Freddy might be a little more hidden with some Spanish moss from a tree close by as he looks down on the shrimp boat where children often play. He loves to swing but his swing is a little different from the one you might use on a playground. Can you spot it up high?

 Franny can see the picnic tables by the pavilion from her hiding place. She is always ready to go on a picnic herself to enjoy her favorite foods: cupcakes, potato salad, BBQ chips, watermelon and lemonade.

FUN FACT

Girl fiddler crabs have two little claws which give them an advantage over the boy fiddler crabs who have the one large claw. The two little claws make eating much easier for the girls, so Franny can really enjoy her picnic!

Franny and Freddy's location will take you just a bit off Calhoun Street. At the corner of Lawton and Calhoun Street, head east on Lawton. When you get to Dubois Park, you'll find the sculptures of the twins there.

Franny sits on one of the rafter supports of the pavilion. Freddy is on a special metal swing hanging from the bough of an oak tree near the Little Shrimp Boat which was built as a project by another one of the Hilton Head Island-Bluffton Chamber of Commerce Leadership classes.

While children can play on the swings and the Little Shrimp Boat near Freddy, you can bring along a picnic lunch to enjoy in the pavilion, with Franny looking down.

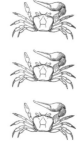

Across the road from Dubois Park is the Martin Family Park, which offers relaxing chairs and picnic tables, and a great big yard to play in. This is the place where the Town of Bluffton displays their Christmas tree in December. If you happen to visit on the first Friday in December, you can witness a lovely and special tree lighting ceremony here at dusk. You will feel like you are in a Hallmark movie! Near Dubois Park is a charming gift shop called Eggs 'n' Tricities, which is full of fashion, jewelry and fun gifts. Also close by is the Woof Gang Bakery, the neighborhood pet store.

The Martin Family Park is named in honor of Ida Martin who started Bluffton's Self Help, an organization that empowers and advocates for Lowcountry neighbors who need help, providing education, training, workforce development, and basic needs. Before she died in 2013, Ida Martin was recognized by President Obama with the Presidential Citizens Medal for her volunteer work with Bluffton Self Help.

Next to the park is the Heyward House Museum and Welcome Center. The town's only museum is located in a former family residence, a lovely example of early Carolina Farmhouse style. The Bluffton Historical Preservation Society purchased the home in 1998 to offer a lot of information about the town. A book called *A Guide to the History of Bluffton* and many other fun and educational items can be purchased in the gift shop inside.

Fiddler Crab FALALA is the most outgoing fiddler crab of the group! She loves to meet new crabs and invites her friends to sleepovers in her burrow whenever she can. In school, she always looks forward to Art Class, her favorite. She especially likes to do claw painting—you might call it finger painting. FaLaLa's favorite color is orange. And she loves Bluffton artist Amiri Farris whose beautiful work captures the Gullah culture.

Here are some clues to help you find FaLaLa:

 You have to look up to see FaLaLa.

 From her spot on her post, FaLaLa has a great view of the Society of Bluffton Artists also known as SOBA Art Gallery. Check out the beautiful monarch butterfly and underwater scene on the outside of the building! You can stand in front of the monarch butterfly for a fun picture of yourself.

 FaLaLa can see the intersection of Church Street and Calhoun Street from her spot on the post with signs that point the way to Peaceful Henry's, The Cottage Café, and the Bluffton General Store.

FUN FACT

If a Fiddler Crab loses one of its claws, it will grow that claw back!

After you've enjoyed a picnic or time in one of the parks, go back to Calhoun and head north for a stop at the places near FaLaLa. Her sculpture is located on a concrete post on the corner of Church Street and Calhoun.

There are a lot of fun places to visit near FaLaLa. The Society of Bluffton Artists (SOBA) is filled with artwork by local artists. It was founded in 1994, with the mission to "Promote a public interest in, and an appreciation of, visual arts in the community, as well as to assist artists at all levels of development to enhance their artistic abilities in the visual arts."

Just down the street, you will find more art galleries worth exploring. One is the Pluff Mudd Art Gallery, which was built around 1945 as a military housing structure on Hilton Head Island and moved to Bluffton sometime after WWII. There is a piano on the front porch for folks to come by and play.

East on Church Street you will find Jacob Preston Pottery, home to "Bluffton's Tallest Potter." Made from reclaimed materials, this building was previously used as a Baptist church and a school. A sign above the door reads "Bluffton Tabernacle 1945." Next door is the Bluffton General Store, a premier boutique gift shop filled with local art, gifts, candles, coastal inspired home décor, and much more! Next to the General Store is M's another boutique shop.

Across Calhoun Street from FaLaLa's post is the Spartina 449 Flagship Store. Spartina brings fun and beauty to shore inspired clothing, handbags and gifts. Nearby Al and Harry's Home Fashions offer lovely pieces of furniture and lots of other things for your home. The Storybook Shoppe, South Carolina's premier children's bookstore, is also in this area. The owner handpicks all the books inside. Next door is a wonderful shop called The Complete Home which has a lot of unique accessories, gourmet food and art—everything your heart desires to "complete your home"!

Just south of Spartina is a restaurant called The Cottage, a wonderful place for breakfast or lunch. It's quaint and cozy with a scrumptious menu—especially the bakery items. The building was constructed in 1868 by J. J. Carson, who was known for his bravery in saving the life of General Stonewall Jackson during the Civil War.

FERGUSON is the next Fiddler Crab for you to find.

Ferguson loves music and plays the fiddle, of course. His favorite song to play is "If You're Happy and You Know It, Click your Claws!" He is going to try out for the school orchestra next year and is taking violin lessons to learn how to play in a more classical style.

Here are some clues to help you find Ferguson:

 You have to look up high to see Ferguson.

 Ferguson has a great view of The Corner Perk across the street and could jump down and get a glass of iced tea with you—sweet tea, of course!

 Ferguson loves being at the corner of Calhoun Street and May River Road—a great place to watch people.

FUN   FACT

Fiddler Crabs scientific name is Uca Perplexa (pronounced: you-ku per-plex-uh).
They got the name Fiddler Crabs because the big claw on the boys
make it look like they are playing a fiddle!

Ferguson's sculpture is located at the intersection of Calhoun Street and May River Road. Here are pictures of him on top of the road sign.

From this intersection, head on over to The Promenade, which is loaded with fun gift shops and great restaurants, including the Corner Perk Brunch Café and Coffee Roasters is across the street from this fiddler. Look for the big Oyster Shell outside of the coffee shop decorated with all the musical instruments. By now you have likely spotted a lot of big oyster shells that are a part of "The Shell Art Trail" in Bluffton. Many businesses display these uniquely painted giant oyster shells created by local artists. This public art trail will entertain and educate. Upstairs from the Corner Perk is The Roasting Room where some awesome musicians play…and you already know that Fiddler Crab Ferguson loves that!

The Town of Bluffton Annual Christmas parade travels from Bridge Street to Calhoun and turns west on May River Road at this intersection. A typical year brings huge crowds to town for this popular event, with many bands, floats, and groups marching along the parade route. The year 2021 marked the 50th anniversary of this amazing extravaganza presented by the Town of Bluffton.

Just down the street is a restaurant called "Farm," which sources locally from fishermen and farmers for its seasonally inspired menu items.

FLETCHER is the next Fiddler Crab for you to find.

Fletcher is the youngest crab of the group and wanted to be close to his teacher, Mr. Finnegan. He enjoys studying geography and likes to look at maps, which is why he's hiding in the spot he found. Fletcher's hiding place outlines the geography of the original one square mile of Old Town Bluffton.

Here are some clues to help you find Fletcher:

 Fletcher is near a brick map showing Old Town Bluffton. Look closely and you just might see some clues about where all the fiddler crabs are.

 You can see Fletcher from the 4-corner area kitty-corner across from Nickel Pumpers.

 Fletcher is sitting on a sign about Fiddler Crabs.

FUN FACT

Fiddler Crabs only need about 2 to 3 inches of water to exist,
and they like the temperature to be between 74 and 80 degrees.

Fletcher sits on another "Follow the Fiddlers" sign at the corner of Bluffton and May River Roads, a short walk east from Calhoun. The locals call that intersection Four Corners.

The plaza reproduces the map of the Historic District, with red bricks defining the original one-square mile area and darker color bricks for the streets. Just behind this inlay map is Tom Herbkersman Commons, with a shaded park bench to enjoy the scenery.

At a nearby restaurant, Nectar Farm Kitchen, you can get dishes prepared with ingredients made and grown in the Lowcountry. And Old Town Bluffton Inn provides visitors with an elegant, special place to stay in the heart of the Historic District.

Across the street from Fletcher is the Cornerstone Church. In the spring the azaleas around this church are gorgeous!

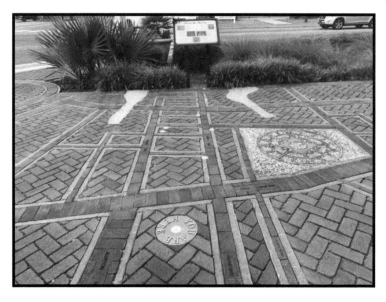

To the south on Boundary Street is the beautiful historic Campbell Chapel African Methodist Episcopal (AME) Church, which was built by white Methodists in 1853. Twenty years later in 1874, nine African American freedmen, who had probably been slaves of members of the white congregation, purchased it. They started to alter the building and expand the site as the church grew. It's likely that they installed the cast-iron bell that is currently visible in the cupola. Today, Campbell Chapel AME continues to provide a space where congregants can educate youth, worship freely, and participate in outreach ministries. The building was listed in the National Register of Historic Places on April 26, 2019.

The teacher, MR. FINNEGAN is the last Fiddler Crab for you to find.

Mr. Finnegan makes sure everyone stays on time during recess and keeps watch to make sure
   all the Fiddler Crabs find their way back to the May River. He loves teaching the Fiddler Crab
   History Class and especially likes the history of Old Town Bluffton.

Here are some clues to help you find Mr. Finnegan:

 Mr. Finnegan is located in The Promenade and is farthest away from the May River.

 Mr. Finnegan is hanging around a community sign board.

 You can see Mr. Finnegan if you are walking on the State of Mind Street near
   Bluffton BBQ, Captain Woody's, Local Pie and Agave Restaurants.

FUN FACT

Fiddler Crabs molt about every eight weeks.
This means that as they grow their outer shell peels off to reveal their new shell.

While you are now at the corner of Boundary and May River Road, head north on Boundary (also called Bluffton Road or 46) for your last crab stop. The sculpture of Mr. Finnegan, the fiddler crabs' teacher, let his sculpture sits on the community sign board.

There are many amenities to check out in The Promenade. Although this area does not have any historic sites, like most of the others, the shops, restaurants and businesses have a similar look and feel as the rest of Old Town Bluffton. The reason is that, from 2005 to 2006, the town government, a group of citizens, and a planning firm worked together to create a blueprint for the future development of Bluffton, with the goal of maintaining the uniqueness of Old Town and reflect its eclectic character. Following the Master Plan since then has been successful in preserving Bluffton's distinctive ambiance and resulted in the area now called The Promenade.

After the long walk you might be hungry or ready to visit some of the wonderful restaurants or shops in The Promenade. No matter which one you choose, you will not be disappointed!

There are a lot of shops where you can purchase fun and unique things. Some of those shops are Lettrs Gifts, Cocoon, The Haven Boutique, J. McLaughlin, and the lovely Garden Gate Nursery.

Some of the eateries are: Sippin' Cow Cafe and Grill, Cork's Wine, The Bluffton Room (*picture left*), and Calhouns Street Tavern. Across from the community sign board where this fiddler crab is located, you'll find more restaurants serving Lowcountry goodness, notably Captain Woody's, Agave, Local Pie, and Bluffton BBQ.

Well, that was quite a trek finding the sculptures of the Fiddler Crabs in Mr. Finnegan's class. FULTON, FELIX, FALALA, FREDDY, FLETCHER, FRANNY, FERGUSON, FELICIA, FRANKLIN and MR. FINNEGAN hope you found all of them and enjoyed seeing some fun and interesting places in Bluffton along the way.

They're wondering:

 Which is your favorite fiddler crab? (Don't worry, the others won't feel hurt because you didn't pick them.)

 Why did you choose him or her?

 Which fiddler crab was the most difficult to find?

 Which location did you like the most? And why?

Meanwhile, the whole crew and their teacher are back in the water enjoying supper. They hope you had a good time and want you to come back soon!

Bye for now!

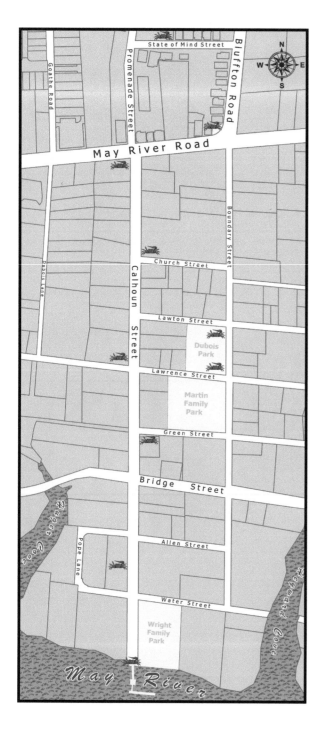

Not every shop and restaurant in Bluffton made its way into these pages, but many did, as you now know. Plan a day, or more, for your next visit in the Historic District, and you will discover plenty of additional, wonderful things about Bluffton along the other downtown streets.

The Pocket Park is tucked away at the south end of Pritchard Street and has beautiful views of the May River. At the southern end of Wharf Street is the Oyster Factory Park and Bluffton Oyster Company where you will find the freshest oysters, shrimp, crabs and fish. The gorgeous dock and park are located next to the Garvin-Garvey Freedman's Cottage which is a restored freed slave's home built around 1870. The exhibit of before-and-after pictures of the cottage are amazing!

A massive oak tree known as "The Secession Oak" has its own history in Bluffton and was located a short distance from the Oyster Factory Park. The 300-plus-year-old tree was thought to be the birthplace of the "Bluffton Movement" which sparked early discussion to secede from the Union. It was under this tree in 1844 that Congressman Robert Barnwell Rhett declared to a crowd that it was time for South Carolina to secede if Congress did not nullify the tariff of 1842. Sadly, a large part of the tree fell in February 2021 resulting in many social comments and even an "obit-tree-ary" for the historic oak.

Most all of the places you've just visited, walked by, or read about are in the Historic District of Bluffton. If you have time and venture out of Bluffton's original square mile, you'll find much more to discover in this quaint and charming town known as the Heart of the Lowcountry.

A short drive will get you to the Burnt Church Distillery which is a business with a heart for Bluffton and who celebrates the rich history of this town. It is recommended as a place to visit for fine local spirits and where you can engage with history. A large piece of the fallen Secession Oak is displayed just inside the front door! The Burnt Church Distillery is helping shape a brighter future as they contribute to the Lowcountry Legacy Fund and different charities each month.

The Secession Oak

A lot of additional information and resources are available at the Heyward House Museum and Welcome Center on Boundary Street.

Heyward House Museum

ACKNOWLEDGMENTS

Thanks to Hilton Head Island-Bluffton Chamber of Commerce Leadership Class of 2015 for creating "Follow the Fiddlers" in Bluffton, South Carolina which inspired this book.

Class members: Diane Bartlett, Kent Berry, Donald Scott Chandler, Nick Kristoff, Christina Marion, Kevin Quat, Lori Ross, Catherine Scarminach Lewallen, Erin Schumacher, Julie Serafino, Brad Tadlok, Janet Turley.

Thank you to Susie Chisholm for creating the lovely Fiddler Crab Sculptures.

Thanks to the following young editors who read, or had read to them, *The Crabs on Calhoun* manuscript. I love that these little readers have given their seal of kid approval to this book. Much appreciation to the children, their parents, grandparents and others!

Hardesty Grandchildren: Grace, Emma, Rilee, Annabelle, Elijah, Caroline, Calvin, Jacob, Michael and Ruth *

June and Claire Ofsansky * Jack Tuten * David Roth * Harrison Chapman * Hannah Piers * Ellie McIlwee *

Cameron Moore * Abigail and Elizabeth Chandler * Terry Lee Webb * Henry Alexander Doughty-Machogu *

Giada and Marin Carge * Wyatt Sunday * Ava, Emme and Otto Vitz * Madeline and Benjamin Lewis *

Miley Swearingen * Connor and Graham Ferguson * Willa Isaacs * Delilah, Amelia and Luke Forster *

Michael Rodriguez * Emerson and Ashton Scott * Eloise LaBruce * Paul Edgerton.

Much gratitude and love to the Town of Bluffton and its Mayor, Council and Staff.

Always thanks to Chris Angermann for his guidance and editing.

Born and raised in Indiana, **Katherine Robinson** departed the Midwest in the early 1980s and called the west coast of Florida her home for many years. After working in Human Resources for banks and municipalities, she moved to Bluffton to run the HR department there. She got the idea for this book when the 2015 Chamber of Commerce Leadership Class created the "Follow the Fiddlers" display of bronze fiddler crabs as their class project. She was enchanted by them and wanted to bring them to life with a story. She always points out the fiddlers to friends and families visiting the area and is happy to guide tours on request. You can contact her at *www.onthehalfshell.shop* website or at her email *Katherine@onthehalfshell.shop*.

Jacob Eaton is an artist, musician and actor, currently resides in Indianapolis, Indiana. In his free time (of which he doesn't have a lot), he enjoys cooking, cinema, and composing music. Jacob has a degree in Fine Arts with a focus on Illustration. His works span from business logos to coloring books, public murals, and galleries. *The Crabs on Calhoun* is his first children's book.

For further information
go to

www.onthehalfshell.shop

CPSIA information can be obtained
at www.ICGtesting.com
Printed in the USA
BVHW091154280422
634389BV00001B/3